THE THREE LIVES OF MAUL ENTRINGER

GRETA GORSUCH

WAYZGOOSE PRESS

CONTENTS

A note on language   v

1. My Third Life, June 19, 1934   1
You Meet Me

2. My First Life, 1904-1921   4
A Child's Life

3. My First Life, 1904-1921   7
I Begin Work

4. My First Life, Monday, May 30, 1921   10
In an Elevator

5. My First Life, Monday, May 30 and Tuesday, May 31, 1921   13
I go to Jail

6. My First Life, Monday, May 30 and Tuesday, May 31, 1921   15
I Leave Tulsa

7. My First Life Ends, June 1, 1921   18
Onion Sacks

8. In Between   19
The Bright People

9. My Second Life Begins, June 1, 1921   21
I am Changed

10. My Second Life, 1921-1926   24
Garnet Train Station

11. My Second Life, 1921-1926   27
I Hear from Mr. Greene

12. My Second Life, 1921-1926   30
Another Letter from Tulsa

13. My Second Life, 1921-1926   32
I Meet Mabel

14. My Second Life, 1921-1926   35
Our Life Together

15. My Second Life, 1921-1926   38
We Move to Wellington

16. My Third Life, June 19, 1934   40
A Belt Buckle

17. My Second Life, June, 1926   42
A New Truck

18. My Second Life Ends, October 31, 1926   45
The Blue Norther

19. My Second Life Ends, October 31, 1926   48
I Fight for my Life

20. In Between   50
Lucky Jack Entringer

21. In Between   52
Uncle Jack Talks

22. In Between   54
Uncle Jack Tells me What to do

23. My Third Life, November? 1926?   57
First Morning

24. My Third Life, November 1, 1926   60
A Broken Bridge

25. My Third Life, November 1, 1926   63
Mrs. Wright Makes Breakfast

26. My Third Life, 1926-1934   66
The Sheriff of Tucumcari

27. My Third Life, 1926-1934   69
Mabel

28. My Third Life, 1926-1934   71
The Great Depression

29. My Third Life, 1926-1934   73
Ghost Beads

30. My Third Life, 1926-1934   76
Dark Night

31. My Third Life, June 20, 1934   79
I Get in my Truck and Go

Epilogue   80

Author's Note   81
Books in This Series   85

A NOTE ON LANGUAGE

This story is set during the 1920s and the 1930s in the southern USA. During this time, the words *colored*, *Negro*, and *nigger* were used to talk about people who were African-Americans. These words are used in the story. However, in modern times, they are considered offensive and are no longer used in everyday speech or writing.

Some of the talk between characters is regional and true to Oklahoma, Texas, and New Mexico of that time, and some would say, in the present day as well.

CHAPTER 1

MY THIRD LIFE, JUNE 19, 1934
YOU MEET ME

My name is Maul Entringer. Yes, that's right. Maul. M-A-U-L. EN-trin-ger. Maul Entringer. Yes, I know Maul's an odd name.

My ma and pa just liked the sound of it. So that's the name they gave me. "Maaaullll?" my ma would shout from our front door. "Where are you? There won't be any dinner for you, if you don't get here right now!" I can still hear her, clear as day. The night falling, her voice strong as a church bell. When she called out my name like that, I knew I should get home, and fast.

Have you ever met anyone who lived three times? Because I have. I have…what? The "what?" could have two answers. One: I have…met someone who lived three times? Yes. I've met one more person like me. Maybe there are more. But I've met just one. He was an old man in Farmington, New Mexico. Two: I have…lived three times? Yes. I have lived three times.

My first life was from 1904 to 1921. That life ended in the back of a truck under sacks of onions. My second life was from 1921 to 1926. That life was a short one! I wanted it to be longer, but it wasn't. It ended by the side of a river. My third life began in 1926. No end date yet. Do I have more time on this third life? I want it to be so.

Stay with me a bit. I'm going to tell you things. You're going to find out where I grew up. You'll hear about my uncle Lucky Jack Entringer, and his strange gift to me. I'll tell you about my beautiful wife, Mabel. You'll hear about Buddy Mills. Even now, I hate to talk about that big mistake of a white man, but I'll do it. I killed him, you see. You'll also hear about Mew, a little gray cat, who found me in New Mexico.

Mew is with me now. She has a little bed on the seat of my truck made out of an Indian blanket. During our long drives she sleeps or sits up and watches the road ahead. It stretches miles and miles into the distance.

Why am I telling you this? What's so special about my three lives? Well, don't you want to know how it all happened? What it was like? As to *why* three lives were given me, I have no idea. I'm sure you want to know why. *I* want to know why. But that is way beyond me.

I'll tell you what I *do* know. It's 1934. I'm on this third life of mine. I disappeared in 1926. But now I want to be found. I want that so badly. I want to go back, and find my beautiful wife, my beautiful Mabel. Will she know me? Will she forgive me? Will she believe how sorry I am? Will she listen when I tell her what made me go, and what made me stay gone?

Tonight, I sit by a small camp fire. It's a soft summer night. There are lots of stars out and there isn't much wind. I'm in a protected spot by the side of a small, slow river. If you must know, it's not far from where my second life ended, in 1926. You'd think I would stay away. It's strange how peaceful this place is.

The sound of the river is very quiet. I sit on a warm blanket with a hot drink. Mew left around sunset. She just slipped into the tall green grasses. She's out hunting for whatever she can find. Sometimes it's a mouse, or a small snake. A few times, she's brought back *things* like a lady's glove or a child's toy or, once, a string of blue beads. I have no idea where she found those. Anyway, if she doesn't find anything to eat tonight, I have some extra food for her.

Here is Mew now. She has something in her mouth. It's not a mouse. She drops it on the blanket in front of me. She steps back, licking her neat gray paws. I pick the thing up. It's dirty and rusted, but I can see it clearly. It's a big man's belt buckle. I know whose it is. Buddy Mills'.

CHAPTER 2

MY FIRST LIFE, 1904-1921

A CHILD'S LIFE

I grew up in Tulsa, Oklahoma. My first memories of my first life were there. My memories were those of a child's, because that is what I was. My family was Ma, Pa, my sister Teeny and my brother Ulysses. I was the middle child. Everyone paid attention to Ulysses, who was oldest, and to Teeny, who was youngest. No one paid attention to me, right in the middle.

Teeny was the cutest little thing. She had a yellow Sunday dress that Ma made for her, for church. Teeny stood still while Ma sat behind her and put white ribbons in her hair. I could never stand still like that. I was quick and skinny. I was always getting up and looking at things—stones in our back garden, a tom cat living under our house, newspapers Pa kept at his store.

Ma thought I got away with things. I wasn't so sure about that. When I was a kid, I did things, like get in a fight with Ulysses. Or I'd help myself to an apple sitting on the kitchen table.

"Didn't you know that apple was my *lunch* at work?" Ma

said. "I'm cleanin' white peoples' houses all day, and now I gotta be hungry while I'm doin' it?"

Ma cleaned and cooked for a white family. Then she would eat anything extra, like half a sandwich, or a little soup left in the pan. She loved apples. If her white family ate everything she made for their lunch, an apple in her pocket was just the thing. Anyway, I felt bad, so I never did anything like that again. That didn't stop me from getting yelled at many, many more times.

I was just a wild kid, without any cares in the world. I got a talking to just about every day. Talking back to teacher. My hand slapped and a talking to. Taking little Rosie Greer's book and hiding it. Rosie calling me "a no good thief" (Ow...*that* hurt.). Leaving dirty hand prints on the towel by the kitchen sink. The back of my head whopped by Pa's big hand *and* a talking to.

We lived in Greenwood. It was a little corner of Tulsa. Hundreds of us black folks lived there, and called it home. Greenwood was close to the trains, and to work. We had our own houses, our own schools, our own churches, and our own businesses. Pa had a hardware store. He was partners with his little brother, Lucky Jack Entringer. They sold hammers, nails, wood, chicken feed, and window glass. Mostly, black folks came to the store but sometimes whites did too. Tulsa was an oil town. It was growing like crazy.

Pa was a big, quiet man. He kept the store's books and handled the money. Selling was my uncle's thing. Pa said Lucky Jack could sell the legs off of a chair. Lucky Jack Entringer was smaller than Pa. He moved and talked fast. He dressed fancy with dark slacks and a white shirt.

He knew just when a customer was about to leave the store. He would go over all friendly. After a few minutes,

Lucky Jack had a sale. If a customer wanted to build a fence, Lucky Jack sold him the wood for it. Then he went over and helped the customer build the fence.

Later, as I got to be 12 or 13, Uncle Jack sent Ulysses and me to help customers with anything they bought hardware for. On any day under the hot Oklahoma sun, you could see us putting a new door on a house or repairing a broken window, all with Entringer Hardware Store goods.

On days when we went to work on a white person's house, Pa talked to Ulysses and me. Pa said, "Just get the job done. Then come back here. Say 'please' and 'thank you' and 'sir' and 'ma'am.' And if anyone offers to pay you, you say 'All paid up, sir. It's not necessary.'"

Pa always looked us in the eye. He said, "It's different outside of Greenwood. Don't forget that. If someone calls out to you on the street, just nod friendly like and *keep walking*."

At first I thought Pa was talking to Ulysses. Then I saw Pa was talking to me. It was like Pa knew trouble would come to me. He was right.

CHAPTER 3

MY FIRST LIFE, 1904-1921
I BEGIN WORK

My memories became those of a young man. I left childhood. Ulysses finished high school, got married, and moved into his own little house just on the edge of Greenwood. He worked for Pa and Lucky Jack. He wanted to learn the hardware store business, and then start his own, maybe in Kansas City or some bigger place. Not long after, I left school. I was 16. Ma argued with me about it. She said, "You gotta stay and finish high school! How many years have I cooked and cleaned for the Jones? That's 'cause I didn't get past 4th grade!"

I answered back, "I want to help out here. Maybe you won't have to cook and clean for other families, then." Ma just shook her head and turned away. Later, I thought how different things might have turned out if I had stayed in school like Ma said.

I worked for Pa and Uncle Jack. For paid work, I kept an eye out for anything I could do. Working in Tulsa, outside of Greenwood, paid the best. Lucky Jack Entringer knew everyone in and out of Greenwood. He helped me find paid work. I learned how to shine shoes for the rich men who worked in those tall office buildings in downtown Tulsa. I washed windows for the big department store on Archer Street. Uncle Jack taught me how to drive. Pretty soon I was driving a taxi cab part time. Once I drove an old white man all the way to Broken Arrow. It was just a little farming village an hour away on bad roads. The old man had a lot of packages to carry. He didn't want to wait for the train. In truth, I think he just wanted someone to talk to. His name was Mr. Bowles, I remember. He had a snowy white beard. He found me someone in Broken Arrow who wanted a ride back to Tulsa. That was kind. That made me a little extra money. My family needed it.

Like I said, Tulsa was an oil town. Sometimes people had money from oil strikes. And sometimes, there weren't any oil strikes, or the price of oil dropped. That meant not as much money for whites and blacks alike. During one bad down-turn, Ma's white family left town for good. That meant less work for her. Secretly I was happy about it. She needed to rest sometimes. Her feet were hurting a lot, I remember. I was helping out as much as I could with the different jobs I had. Money wasn't too bad, even when Pa's store made less.

The one kind of work I could always count on was shining shoes. I got to know two rich white men in a tall downtown building. Mr. Spaulding bought and sold land and oil leases. Mr. Greene owned the taxi company I sometimes drove for. By the time I had to leave Tulsa, he was looking to buy trucks. He wanted to get work from the oil fields, trucking hardware and pipes and goods from the train tracks to the oil wells. He told me, "In a few months, let's try you out driving a truck. It'll be good money!" In the meantime, I took a sack to each man's office. They put in two or three pairs of shoes they needed shined. I'd take them home, shine them, and then bring them back later that day.

It turns out that Uncle Jack had business dealings with Mr. Spaulding. Quietly, Uncle Jack was buying land south of Tulsa. There wasn't any oil drilling there yet, but he thought there might be. So did Mr. Spaulding. Uncle Jack sold oil leases to Mr. Spaulding. Both Uncle Jack and Mr. Spaulding hoped there would be drilling, and then some rich oil strikes. If that happened, there could be quite a lot of money out of it. I didn't know this but Uncle Jack had put my name on his land, and the leases he sold. This was one part of Lucky Jack Entringer's gift to me. The next part was to come on May 31, 1921, when my first life ended.

CHAPTER 4

MY FIRST LIFE, MONDAY, MAY 30, 1921

IN AN ELEVATOR

That Monday I had only one thought. *Rosie Greer. I get to see her tonight.* My heart beat a little faster just thinking about it. Little Rosie Greer, my fourth grade classmate, had grown up pretty. At 17, she was still tiny. Her eyes were still sharp. She wore glasses, but I thought they made her look even smarter. She still loved books. She was working at a bookstore just outside Greenwood. I was on my way to downtown Tulsa with a sack of shoes to take to Mr. Greene. I ran across the street from Greenwood to Tulsa right by the bookstore where Rosie worked. I wasn't watching like I should. I almost got hit by a truck on its way to the train yard. The driver honked his horn and yelled. That caught Rosie's notice and she came to the door with some books in her hand.

She called out, "Maul Entringer, getting into trouble *still?*"

I turned around. Then I saw this tiny beautiful young woman in a blue dress and white shoes, just like she was ready for church. I ended up talking to her. *She* ended up agreeing to meet me that night. The Mount Zion Baptist church was having a little sale of cakes. The money would help build a school for children in Broken Arrow. It wasn't much of a town. I knew that from driving old Mr. Bowles there in a taxi. There were enough black children for their mas and pas to want a school for them. The whites weren't going to build it for them.

The bookstore owner, a white woman in a black dress, told Rosie to get back inside and get to work. Rosie Greer smiled and said "Yes ma'am."

I walked pretty fast into Tulsa. It seemed like no time that I was at the front entrance of Mr. Greene's office building. Mr. Greene was on the seventh floor. Up until now, I just walked up the big stairs. Then I remembered the building had a new elevator. I'd never been in an elevator and I wanted to try it.

I found the elevator at the back of the building. A white man was waiting for the elevator and I waited, too. The big gold doors opened and the man walked in. I followed. I had no idea what to do. Then I noticed a white woman standing there. She was the elevator operator. She wore a little brown jacket and a hat, and a lot of make-up. The white man said to her, "Third floor." She repeated in a high voice, "Third floor, sir."

I thought I should do the same. I said, "Ma'am, seventh floor please." She said nothing, didn't even turn to look at me.

I saw now that the elevator operator was just a girl. She was maybe my age, about 17. The elevator door closed and she pulled at something. The elevator gave a huge JERK up. The white man fell against the wall and said, "Have a care, now!" "Yes sir," said the girl elevator operator.

At the third floor we came to a fast stop. The doors banged open. The man almost ran out of the elevator. The girl operator was new at her job, or something. She wasn't very good at working elevators. Then the elevator doors shut again. As soon as that happened, I knew my mistake. I should have gotten out on the third floor. Now I was alone with a white girl in an elevator. That is something a black boy can never, ever do.

The elevator jerked UP again. When we got to the seventh floor, the girl pulled very hard on something and the elevator came to a fast STOP. As it did so, I fell a little. The girl wasn't so lucky. She fell flat on her face. Without thinking I reached down to help her up. She looked at my hand and cried out as if she had seen something that scared her to death. I pulled my hand back and said, "Sorry." The elevator door opened and I walked out. I just wanted to get Mr. Greene's shoes back to him and get out of there. Back in the elevator, the white girl started to scream.

CHAPTER 5

MY FIRST LIFE, MONDAY, MAY 30 AND TUESDAY, MAY 31, 1921

I GO TO JAIL

Mr. Greene's office door opened. Mr. Greene put his head out and asked, "What in the world?"

The white elevator operator was still screaming. She yelled, "He touched me! He touched me! That nigger touched me! He *attacked* me!"

Mr. Greene asked, "Maul? What's goin' on?"

I couldn't even speak. I just held his bag of shoes out for him to take. He took them, and gave me $4. The whole time the girl kept screaming. Then she started crying, loud as anything. The elevator doors stayed open. She wasn't going anywhere. Pretty soon more office doors opened and white men, along with a few white women, came out into the hall.

Mr. Greene said to me, "You stay here. Let me see what all the noise is about." He walked down the hall to the elevator. A few men followed him. Mr. Greene put his head inside the elevator and talked to the girl. You could still hear her crying.

Mr. Greene came back. The other folks looked in the elevator and then at me. "Maul," he said, "You didn't touch her did you?"

"No!" I said. "The elevator jerked, and she fell."

Down the hall I could see a white man walk fast to his office. Mr. Greene said, "He goin' off to telephone the police. You come in my office. There's goin' to be trouble, if that white girl says you touched her. You let me talk to the police, alright? We'll get it straightened out. I know that girl. She's just young an' silly, is all."

Mr. Greene was right about the police. It wasn't twenty minutes before they came to Mr. Greene's door to take me away. Mr. Greene said, "Come on now! I know this boy's family. He didn't touch that girl. The elevator jerked, an' she fell and got scared."

One police officer, a big white man with red hair, spat on the floor. "Sure," he said, pulling my hands tight behind me. He tied them tight. It hurt. "Come on," he said. "We're going to the station." He got me down the stairs and into a police car. There was already a crowd of people in front of the office building. *How did they get here so fast?* I thought.

CHAPTER 6

MY FIRST LIFE, MONDAY, MAY 30 AND TUESDAY, MAY 31, 1921

I LEAVE TULSA

What happened next in Tulsa I only know because Mr. Greene told me. Within two hours, The *Tulsa Tribune* had the headline: **"Nab Negro for Attacking Girl in Elevator."** By 7 PM that night just about everyone, black and white, knew I had been in the elevator with that white girl. The whites thought I had attacked her.

Actually, not all white folks thought that. The police didn't believe her. A small dark-haired detective told me so when he came to my jail cell at the police station.

"I think she just wanted attention," he said. "She's bad news, according to her ex-husband. Probably trying to get him back. We just need to hold you a bit longer. Things are getting ugly out there."

By "things are getting ugly" he meant that a large mob of white men were outside the jail. They had guns and baseball bats. They believed I had attacked the girl, no matter what the police said. At the same time, the blacks of Greenwood thought the whites would break into the jail, drag me out, and then kill me. A large mob of *them* came to the jail. Within minutes the two crowds, white against black, black against white, began to shout and fight. It was so loud I could hear it inside the jail. I heard a few gun shots.

I was scared for my family. They must be wondering where I was. I was about to call from my jail cell that I wanted to get word to my family, when the door to the cells opened. Uncle Jack was there with Mr. Greene and the dark-haired detective. The detective unlocked the cell.

"What's going on?" I asked. "Are Ma and Pa OK?"

I'd never seen Lucky Jack Entringer look so serious. Now I got really frightened.

"Come on, now," Uncle Jack said. "We need to get you out of here. We've got a truck in back of the jail, outside."

I noticed then Uncle Jack had black stuff all over his clothes. He smelled like smoke! Was there a fire? He pulled me out of the cell and they got me down the stairs. I kept asking questions and finally Mr. Greene shushed me. "We're gettin' you out of here. We're savin' your life. Now hush up."

When we got outside it was dark. It was a little quieter behind the jail. If we were lucky, no one would see us. Uncle Jack pushed me into the back of a farm truck. There were two big piles of sacks with a space in between. Were those sacks of onions? Or potatoes? I couldn't tell.

"Lay down in that little space I made for you there," he said. "We've got to hide you." Then I saw an orange glow in the sky. There *was* a fire. *Oh my god*, I thought, *Tulsa is burning*.

As if he read my mind, Uncle Jack said, "That's Greenwood burning. Not Tulsa. Your ma and pa are OK. I saw them get out. *Listen*. This truck's going to take you to Broken Arrow, get you out of here. White men find you, you'll be dead. Do you see?" He took something from around his neck and put it around mine. I couldn't see it.

"Now lay down," he said. "Let's get these onion sacks around you. Got to hide you." The truck drove off into the night, Mr. Greene at the wheel.

That's the last time I saw Lucky Jack Entringer. At least, in this life.

CHAPTER 7

MY FIRST LIFE ENDS, JUNE 1, 1921

ONION SACKS

I die not long after. Those sacks of onions! As we leave Tulsa, the red from the fires become just a thick darkness. Instead of smoke, I smell dust. We are safely out of Tulsa, but then the truck goes down that terrible road to Broken Arrow. Do you remember me telling you how bad the road is? In the darkness, four of the big onion sacks fall into the little space where I am hiding. They fall right on top of me. I try to get up but the space is too narrow. I try to throw the sacks off. I try to sit up. I can't. I try to use my arms and legs to push the sacks up. But at 30 pounds apiece, I can't do it! It's too much! I can only lay in the darkness. I can't breathe. I can't shout. Even if I could, Mr. Greene can't hear me. The weight pushes down on me. After that, I remember nothing.

CHAPTER 8

IN BETWEEN

THE BRIGHT PEOPLE

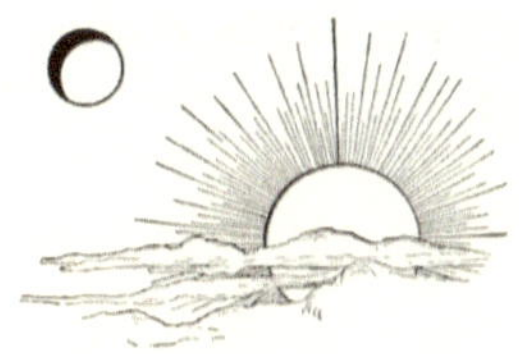

It is not light. It is not dark. It is more like shadows, some darker than others. I am not on my back. I am not standing up. I am just *there*. I can see and hear but I don't know how. I am not walking. I move *forward*. How? I don't know. There is no feeling of weight. I think *At least those onion sacks aren't on me*.

And so I move forward. Then I see something a little brighter in the gray darkness ahead. I move toward it. As I get closer I see four bright shapes. They are like people standing with the brightest possible fire behind them. I can see heads, arms, and legs, but no faces. They stand under a huge tree. I look up, and the tree reaches up into a blackness with small, small lights even further up, beyond the endless tree. *Stars* I think. *Those are stars.*

"Not stars," says a voice. One of the bright shapes is very close to me. "Those are our memories. Those are our lives. Yours too, now."

At these words, something like a bright rocket flies up in the air. It is so bright, and blue and gold and green all at once.

The rocket flies higher and higher until it joins all the small lights in the blackness.

I feel a warm wind on my shoulder. It pushes me around like gentle hands. The bright shapes are close to me now. Soon, they are simply one shape, with me, so bright and warm. I move forward with them and together we are like the sunrise on the edge of the world. Bright, golden, unstoppable, shadows racing ahead.

CHAPTER 9

MY SECOND LIFE BEGINS, JUNE 1, 1921

I AM CHANGED

I was lying on my side. I hurt all over. It didn't help that someone was shaking me hard.

"Ow," I said.

"Hey! Hey Maul!" It was Mr. Greene.

The truck was stopped. My chest opened. I breathed. I rolled over onto my back. I was on the ground. I saw early sunlight through the branches of a huge tree. Mr. Greene helped me sit up. I saw some of the big onion sacks on the ground. I looked around. An old man with a long white beard stood nearby. I knew him.

"Mr. Bowles?" I said. "What are you doing here?"

"What am *I* doing here?" he said in his old man's voice. "This is my place, in Broken Arrow. Mr. Greene here's my sister's boy."

"You scared me there, Maul," Mr. Greene said. He looked ten years older. He'd been driving all night. When he found me under the onion sacks he had a real shock.

Mr. Bowles said, "You should have seen him jump up into

the truck. He found you, and threw off those onion sacks like he was only 20 years old. I never saw the like!" He laughed.

Mr. Greene did not laugh.

"Here, let's see you stand up," Mr. Greene said. I stood up. Mr. Greene stepped back. He said, "Maul?" Then it was like he couldn't speak. His mouth opened and then closed.

I looked down at myself. My clothes were dirty after being in the truck all night. I felt different. Something had changed. I looked down at my feet. Somehow my pants were way too short. They fit perfectly the day before—or was it—*two* days ago I was talking to Rosie Greer in the door of the bookstore? Now the pants hardly covered my knees. My dirty white shirt was the same. It was too tight. It barely covered my elbows. Had I grown? How?

"What…what *happened* to you Maul?" Mr. Greene said. He held his hand to his jaw, like someone had socked him a good one.

"Huh," Mr. Bowles said. "I've got some clothes that'll fit him." And he went into his little white house.

Mr. Greene's hand was still at his jaw, trembling.

"Mr. Greene!" I said. "Are you alright?"

"Yeah," he said. "Maybe I'm just seein' things. It's been a long night. I'm too tired to think straight, I guess." But until he drove away ten minutes later, I saw him looking at me. I made him nervous.

Before he left, he handed me some money and a small piece of paper. He told me Greenwood was completely burned. The fight that started in front of the jail got worse. The whites made their way over to Greenwood. Those black folks would pay! You couldn't let a black boy attack a white girl! They burned every house, every business, and every church. Mr. Greene said that even worse, the newspaper had printed my name and my description. He told me I needed to get out of Oklahoma, and stay out.

"What about my family?" I asked.

"I'll check on 'em when I get back to Tulsa," Mr. Greene said. "Your Pa is smart. I'm sure he got everyone out."

"How will I reach you? Where will I go?" I said. I'd never lived anywhere but Greenwood.

"That piece of paper has the name and address of someone I know in Garnet, Texas." Mr. Greene said. "He has a taxi company. He'll help you out. I'll get word to you there."

"Garnet?" I asked.

Mr. Greene then left. He wanted to get back. He wanted to get away from me, too, I think.

Mr. Bowles came out with some old, clean clothes for me to put on. "Let's get you something to eat," he said. "Then I need to get you to the train station. The sooner you're out of Oklahoma, the better."

I felt something around my neck. I took it off to look at it. It was what Uncle Jack had put around my neck when I left Tulsa. It was just a string of brown seeds. I had never seen him wearing it, but he must have been, all the years I knew him. I rubbed them between my fingers. I smelled something like pine, or cedar. I put the necklace back over my head. It didn't come off again until November 1, 1926.

CHAPTER 10

MY SECOND LIFE, 1921-1926
GARNET TRAIN STATION

By the next afternoon, I was in Garnet, Texas, far west and out of Oklahoma. I began my second life. I got off the train, out of the "colored car." It was raining and windy. There was no waiting room at the train depot for blacks. I found a train worker who let me into the freight office to use his telephone. "Don't be on there long," he said.

I dialed the number of Mr. Greene's friend, Mr. Abram Choat. For a few days, he and his wife took me in, then helped me find a room in a colored boarding house in "The Flats." The Flats was like Greenwood. Only black folks lived there. The Flats was nothing like Greenwood, and Garnet was nothing like Tulsa. Garnet was much smaller. It looked raw. The Flats only had a few hundred of us. There were few black-owned businesses. Just two barbershops, a pool hall, and a few stores for canned goods. There was a church or two.

Mr. Abram Choat owned a taxi business, just like Mr. Greene said. He was happy to learn I could drive a taxi. Almost right away, he wanted to switch me to trucks. "Big strong young man like you can handle a truck," he said. He was right. He had just bought a big Armleder Motor Truck. It was huge, and the thing was the devil to drive. It took all the strength in my new, long arms just to steer it. It was slow and loud, and very hard to stop once it got moving. Pretty soon I was taking truckloads of cotton from the train tracks to "The Compress." Lots of blacks worked there, pressing oil out of cotton seed.

I waited to hear from Mr. Greene about my family. What about Ma, Pa, Teeny, and Ulysses and his wife? The Garnet newspapers were full of the "race riot" in Tulsa. Twenty six blacks were dead, and nine whites. *All* of Greenwood, every bit of it, was gone, burned down. All this for *one* mistake? For me being alone in an elevator with a white girl who just wanted attention? Ma and Pa's house burned down, my old school gone, our homes, our churches, our shops, our movie theaters made into piles of ashes. Even as I started my second life, I felt so empty inside. I couldn't sleep. I wasn't eating. I got thin. Around my fifth week in Garnet, I went to one of the Negro churches. I wanted to be around people.

The women and men of the church welcomed me warmly. They had a "supper club" for new people in town. So, on Wednesday and Sunday nights I went to someone's house for an evening meal. I met a few other new people at supper club including Dr. Chester Hollis from Missouri. He was a medical doctor. Soon, he told me, his wife would join him in Garnet, and bring her sister to help with the move. The sister, Mabel Johnson, was a cook. She was hoping to find work in Garnet, maybe working at one of the new hospitals that had opened up.

Chester told me, "As thin as you are, maybe you should get to know Mabel. She'll get some healthy weight back on you."

I had to laugh. It seems like forever since I had laughed. It felt good. No one asked too many questions. I just said I was from Oklahoma. I was looking for a new start in Texas.

CHAPTER 11

MY SECOND LIFE, 1921-1926
I HEAR FROM MR. GREENE

I finally heard from Mr. Greene. One day in September, when I got to Mr. Abram Choat's office to start work, a letter was waiting for me. I opened it with shaking hands. Mr. Greene wrote that Ma, Pa, Teeny, and Ulysses had left Tulsa for Kansas City, "or maybe St. Louis." Pa's hardware business was gone. Our house was gone. As if that wasn't bad enough, Mr. Greene said that he had "sad news" for me. Lucky Jack Entringer was dead. I stopped reading. It was as though my heart had turned to ice.

It seems that after getting me out of Tulsa, Uncle Jack went to the hardware store to try to save it from the fire. He and some other men succeeded in beating back the flames. Then a mob of white men came. With sticks and rocks, the mob forced Uncle Jack and his friends away from the hardware store. Uncle Jack shouted at the white mob's leader to let him save the store.

According to one of his friends, Uncle Jack yelled at the man, "I know you! I've seen you plenty of times! You've bought plenty of things from me! What's wrong with you? Stop this!"

The mob leader said "Shut up, you." He pulled out a gun and shot Uncle Jack in the chest. Then the hardware store burned down. Uncle Jack's friends tried to find him a doctor to save him, but with the darkness and shouting and burning and mobs, they couldn't.

I spent the next month unable to sleep or eat again. I had no idea what to do with myself. My family was gone. Lucky Jack Entringer, who helped save my life, had been killed by a white mob. I lay in bed, unable to sleep most nights. I often felt for the string of brown seeds around my neck. Sometimes around dawn I might sleep a little. Then I would jerk awake with a bad dream about fire, onion sacks, and a shaky white girl in an elevator. Those times, the string of brown seeds Uncle Jack gave me felt very warm against my skin.

I thought a lot about Uncle Jack. Was it my fault he died? I said that to my friend, Chester. That meant I had to tell him about Tulsa. I had to tell him about that awful day when I made the mistake of staying on an elevator with a girl probably no one should be alone with.

Chester looked at me for a long time. Then he said, "Uh-hmmm. Let me see. A white mob kills dozens of blacks. They burn an entire community. They never go to jail for it. That's *not* your fault. You did nothing wrong."

I put my face in my hands.

Chester was quiet for a little. Then he said, "It sounds to me like your Uncle Jack wanted to help you. That's what family does. It's not *your* fault, and it's not *his* fault that a white mob wanted his store to burn."

Those were hard words. However, I knew they were true. I slept a little better that night. It helped to tell someone what had happened. I decided *not* to tell Chester I had also *died* that night, and that I somehow came back to life six inches taller. I also had the feeling I was a few years older. Like I died at 17 but woke up at 25. But I had no proof of that. I had no idea what Chester, a medical doctor, might say about that.

Mr. Abram Choat, my boss, knew people in Kansas City and in St. Louis.

"I'll get word out to some people. They'll find out if your ma and pa are there. They ought to be able to find them through church groups and such," he said.

Several months went by. No one knew anything about a family called Entringer who had fled Tulsa.

CHAPTER 12

MY SECOND LIFE, 1921-1926
ANOTHER LETTER FROM TULSA

I spent Christmas of 1921 in Garnet. I made friends. I saved money. I worked six days a week driving a truck for Mr. Choat. I was a frequent visitor to the Garnet train station because of my job. I became friendly with the freight man who had let me use his phone my first morning in Garnet. I moved into a better room. This one was in a nice house owned by an older colored woman and her sister. She rented out three rooms to Negro men, and served breakfast and dinner. The house was two streets off the busy main street in "the Flats." It was quieter, and not so dusty.

I think it was February when I got another letter from Tulsa. This time it was from Mr. Spaulding. Mr. Greene had quietly told him where I was.

"My boy, I have news for you," Mr. Spaulding said in his letter. He had done a lot of business with Lucky Jack Entringer over the years, he said. It was a shame what happened last June. He told the police what he had heard about Uncle Jack's death. He also made sure Uncle Jack was buried in a cemetery outside Tulsa. It was called "Dream Land." I could visit his grave later "when things cooled down." He had ordered a stone for Uncle Jack's grave. He was happy to pay for it "to do this one kindness for a friend."

Mr. Spaulding then said, "So far I have given you only sad news. I have something better to tell you, now." He said that Uncle Jack had bought land in my name. Some of that land had oil leases on them. That meant that any oil company that wanted to find oil on the land would have to pay me cash money. The leases weren't worth very much right now. However, they could be, "if they start drilling for oil out there."

Mr. Spaulding then said he had opened a bank account for me in Garnet. He didn't think it was safe for me to come to Tulsa to do any banking. "Anything your land or your oil leases make, I will deposit at the Garnet National Bank. When you become 21 years of age, the money will be yours to do with as you wish," he said.

He ended his letter with "Your uncle thought a lot about the future. I hope you will follow in his footsteps. What happened here in Tulsa is a shame. It's not something anyone will ever forget, white or black. Yours sincerely, Henry Spaulding."

From that moment, I began to live my second life more fully. The past haunted me. My family was gone, at least until I could find them, somehow, somewhere. Uncle Jack was dead. My first life, my childhood, my hopes of that time, were gone—but I was alive. When I turned 21, there were things I wanted to do.

CHAPTER 13

MY SECOND LIFE, 1921-1926
I MEET MABEL

The memories from my second life are those of a man. My hopes and dreams became *plans*. I knew I loved to drive trucks. I loved getting out on the road. Most importantly, I knew something about the world. I figured out how to make my plans real. If I drove a truck for someone else, like Mr. Abram Choat, I could make enough money to live. If I *owned* my own truck, I might make more money. I could build on that and make whatever life I wanted. I had some money now in a bank account in Garnet. It was $280 from Uncle Jack's oil leases. I never spent it. Instead, I kept it and made plans. I still wore Lucky Jack Entringer's brown seed necklace.

The memories from my second life are also sweet. Perhaps this is because my second life was so short. I didn't want to leave it. How hard I fought to hold onto it! But on October 31, 1926, I left it.

The sweetest, most powerful memory of them all is about my wife. I met my beautiful Mabel on New Year's Day, 1924. She was the sister-in-law of my best friend, Dr. Chester Hollis. She had been talking about coming to Garnet for several years.

Mabel told me later that she just never found the chance to leave Missouri. First, her father and mother needed her to stay. Then, she found a good job as a hospital cook. Finally her sister, Mrs. Claire Hollis, wrote in a letter: "Mabel, what's taking you so long? Get out here to Garnet. There are plenty of good jobs here, with two new hospitals. This country is filling up fast. And Mabel--there's a new college opening up!"

It was that last part about the college that got Mabel's attention. It was a white college. Being black, Mabel could not go to it. If one college started up, there might be a "colored" school she could go to. Mabel was big on reading and getting an education. Finally, she traveled from Missouri to Garnet by train "just to spend Christmas." Well, she ended up staying.

Chester and Claire had brought Mabel to church for a special New Year's Day service. Everyone was talking about Mabel.

"Oh, did you see Dr. Hollis' sister-in-law?"

"Oh my, she is turned out so well! What a pretty dress!"

"Did you see her white gloves?"

You could see how the church ladies were looking around for the perfect young man in Garnet for Mabel to marry. I had to laugh. For me, I had no plans to marry. I needed to save more money first. Once I turned 21 in another month, I could use money from my bank account to buy my own truck, or anything else I wanted.

When I saw Mabel in church, I forgot that I had no plans to marry. I forgot to think. I almost forgot to breathe. She was short. She wore a beautiful deep green dress and coat. Mabel told me later she had made the dress herself, and her mother the coat. It looked incredible on Mabel, against her skin. Yes, like the church ladies said, she wore white gloves on her small hands. Her dark wavy hair was pulled back from her face.

What a lovely face! Her skin was perfect. She wore just a hint of make-up, perhaps a little lipstick. I was completely captured by her eyes. Her eyes were large and light brown, a rich honey color. Oh my. Later I learned that Mabel's eyes missed nothing. She noticed everything around her.

I walked over to where she stood with Chester and Claire. I shook Mabel's hand and managed to tell her my name.

She looked up into my eyes and said, "Maul? As in M-A-U-L? What an interesting name. How did you get it?"

"My ma and pa just liked the sound of it," I said.

"Hmm," she said. "It's a good name."

Chester and Claire must have noticed how Mabel had captured me, because they invited me to their house that night for dinner. After that, at least until I died the second time, Mabel and I were never apart.

CHAPTER 14

MY SECOND LIFE, 1921-1926
OUR LIFE TOGETHER

Mabel didn't return to Missouri. Instead, she stayed in Garnet and married me. I used some of my savings and found a nice little house to rent.

"We can build our own house later, maybe in another town," I told her. "We might not stay in Garnet, you know."

Mabel found a job at a new hospital and worked a morning shift from 4 AM to 2 PM. She was such a good baker, and the hospital staff and patients loved her fresh bread.

Mabel and I talked a lot about where to live. We liked our friends in Garnet. We liked our church. In truth, I got tired of living in The Flats. It was the only place blacks were allowed to live. Sure, there were some nice houses here and there. Unfortunately, we were right next to factories that made noise and smoke. It was a dirty part of town. We had to carry water from a central tap at the end of the block. Mabel got tired of that pretty fast. She was from Excelsior Springs, Missouri, where every household, black or white, had indoor water and toilets. She thought Garnet was rough and raw and dirty.

Mabel also thought the whites of Garnet hated blacks. One

afternoon after work she walked home from the hospital. She stopped in a grocery store she knew for some cream. We were having Chester and Claire over that night to play cards. Mabel liked serving strong coffee with fresh cream while we played.

A group of white college boys followed her from the store. They talked about her and how she looked. Mabel walked a little faster. They got closer and closer. Mabel was tired after a long day of work. Her grocery sack was heavy. Finally one of them said, "She's good lookin' for a black gal." Mabel had had enough. She turned, to tell them to leave her alone. Do you remember I said Mabel's eyes missed nothing? Well, she saw one of those boys step back, and look down and away. So she spoke, and looked right at him. She said, "You all have no right to speak to me that way. College is wasted on you!"

At that moment, a police car drove by. Mabel turned and walked home as fast as she could. She looked over her shoulder, thinking those boys would start following her again. I knew what that was like, that looking-over-the-shoulder feeling. I felt it all the time. It was crazy, but sometimes I knew that bad luck would follow me from Tulsa. It was like being haunted by a ghost.

We went to the police to report the boys.

The officer at the police station said, "What do you expect me to do about it? You don't know their names, do you?" Mabel didn't. The officer said, "Then we're done here. Go on, get out." He stepped away and sat down at his desk.

Mabel stayed angry for days. It came to me then that I had never told Mabel about Tulsa. She knew nothing about the part I played in the burning of Greenwood and the disappearance of my family. She didn't know about Lucky Jack Entringer and how he and Mr. Greene saved my life. Would it help or hurt Mabel to know just how bad things could get for

Negroes? Later, I knew in my heart I was wrong not to tell Mabel more about me. It might have changed that horrible mistake I made in my third life.

After our visit to the police, the string of brown seeds around my neck began to feel very warm. I felt for it through my shirt so often that Mabel asked where I got the necklace.

"From my uncle," I said. She just looked at me. It was the first time that I had even mentioned that I had family. Then I said, "I think it's time for a change. Let's find another town."

CHAPTER 15

MY SECOND LIFE, 1921-1926
WE MOVE TO WELLINGTON

I spoke with Mr. Abram Choat. He told me about a town called Wellington. It was a few hours east of Garnet. There was a good highway between Wellington and another town called Childress. Both towns had big train stations. There was a lot of money to be had in towns like that. Farmers grew vegetables, cotton, and corn, and raised cattle and sheep. They needed trucks with drivers to take their produce to the train station to be shipped off as freight to Dallas or some other big city.

Mabel and I made plans to move to Wellington. Mabel seemed happy about it. I closed my bank account in Garnet. We said goodbye to all our friends. The following week, we were in Wellington.

Wellington was much smaller than Garnet. It felt different, too. The pace of life was a little slower. People knew each other, and would stop to talk whether they were walking, on horseback, in a horse-pulled wagon, or in a car. In those days in Wellington, plenty of people still rode horseback. There weren't many Negroes in town, but there were enough of us for a church and five or six black-owned businesses.

Mabel found work fast. Just a month before, a medical doctor had opened a small ten-bed hospital and he needed a cook. As soon as he heard about Mabel's hospital work in Garnet, he hired her on the spot.

We found a small house that we liked and moved in. Mabel and I opened a bank account in Wellington. I sent a letter to Mr. Spaulding to tell him I had moved. I gave him our new savings account number and let him know I was married, now. Any oil lease money belonged to both me and Mabel.

It was June, 1926. I didn't know it then, but my second life was about to end. Would I have done anything differently? I don't know. I do know it was the happiest time of my life. Mabel and I found a little spot we loved, north of town. It had a little river with water and trees and birds and quiet. One golden afternoon when it wasn't too hot we lay down in the shade of a tree by the river. I looked up into the green leaves and branches and felt the world turn quietly beneath me.

CHAPTER 16

MY THIRD LIFE, JUNE 19, 1934
A BELT BUCKLE

I add more wood to my little camp fire. Millions of stars are in the clear night sky. I'm tired, but this quiet summer night is too beautiful to miss. I can sleep later, after my camp fire has died down a little, after I've told you the story I mean to tell. This next part is hard. I'm glad my little cat Mew is here with me. I'm sad and deeply fearful when I think about my second death.

Mew has woken up. She comes over for me to pet her soft gray head. Now Mew walks silently around our little camp, always at the edge of the light the camp fire makes. She looks out into the night. She sniffs at something I can't smell. Maybe a deer? A skunk? A coyote? I heard a few coyotes singing earlier.

I hold Buddy Mills' dirty, rusted belt buckle in my hand. I turn it over and over. It's been outdoors in the sun and rain and wind for eight years now. You can hardly tell it's even a belt buckle. When Mew dropped it onto my camp blanket, I knew what it was and who it belonged to. A dead man.

All right then. If I don't tell you what happened now, I never will. I want to tell this story only once. Then I'm done.

CHAPTER 17

MY SECOND LIFE, JUNE, 1926
A NEW TRUCK

A few weeks after Mabel and I moved to Wellington, I made a decision. I was ready to buy my own truck. Now, Mr. Abram Choat had given me the name of a man in Wellington who wanted to hire a truck driver. I worked for Mr. Loudermilk for several months. Driving his truck I would visit small farms and ranches around Wellington. The farmer and two or three of his kids would load up their onions or pumpkins into the truck and I would drive everything to the train station. I got to know quite a few of the farmers and ranchers in the area. One rancher, Mr. Wright, had a sick wife. He didn't have anyone to help him load his sheep onto the truck, so I took off my jacket and helped him. Oh, that was hard, dirty work! Mr. Wright offered me some water to drink and to wash my hands with. My wife Mabel, always thinking about others, sent a loaf of fresh bread for Mrs. Wright on my next trip out there.

I was happy for the work, and happy to drive Mr. Loudermilk's truck. I wanted to make my own money now. I thought I could do that if I found the right truck to buy. Then I could set my own prices for carrying onions or pumpkins or cotton from one place to another.

It took a few months, but I found a used truck that was exactly what I wanted. A local farmer, Mr. Hiram Mills, had a Model-T Ford truck he had bought new two years before. He wanted to buy some more land for his farm, and he needed cash money. I went out to his farm to look at the truck. He had the truck in a barn to keep it out of the weather. It was black, like all Model-T Fords. It was a good farm truck. It was high up off the ground. You had to climb up into the cab to get inside to drive the thing. Out on these farm roads you could get into deep mud. With the truck so high up, you had a good chance of driving through the mud and not getting stuck. As Mr. Abram Choat once told me, "Those Model-Ts, they're small, but they can take the roads out here!"

Mr. Mills had kept the Model-T in good shape. It started up right away. The tires looked okay. The cab of the truck, the front part, had a roof. It had two doors, one on the driver's side and one on the passenger's side. The back of the truck, the truck bed, was extra-long. I could carry quite a bit back there. I could never truck cattle, the Model-T was too small for that. I could take five or six sheep, or a pretty big load of cotton or some other freight.

We agreed on a price. He said he'd bring the truck into town the next day. I went to the bank, and got out the money I needed from my savings account. We would meet at the Wellington town square. It sounds simple, doesn't it? Wrong.

On the day of the truck sale, there was trouble thanks to Buddy Mills, that big mistake of a man. Mr. Hiram Mills had a son, and that was Buddy. Buddy was a tall guy with bad teeth. He was what...20? And his skin still bad like a teenager's. It turns out Buddy wanted the truck for himself. He was mad at his pa, Mr. Mills, for selling me the truck.

"Pa," he said, "Don't sell our truck to that nigger." That word. I won't answer to it.

"Hush. I'm done talking about it," said Mr. Mills. He counted the cash money I gave him. Then, he handed me the papers for the truck. All the while, Buddy Mills was red in the face, and silent. His eyes moved back and forth from me, to Mr. Mills, and then back to me. He watched as Mr. Mills put the $185 cash money into his pocket. Then Buddy asked, "Where does a nigger get cash money like that anyway?" Mr. Mills ignored him. So I did, too. Maybe that was a mistake.

CHAPTER 18

MY SECOND LIFE ENDS,
OCTOBER 31, 1926

THE BLUE NORTHER

The day starts out good. I say goodbye to Mabel. I kiss her. Her cheek is soft. Then I pick up a load of cotton from a farm thirteen miles north of town. I'm supposed to take it to the freight train at Shamrock, another sixteen miles north. Instead, I decide to drive home to Wellington, which is south and out of my way. I've got to drive slow. The cotton is heavy. The highway is not paved. It's just dirt.

The weather has been warm and sunny, and the roads dry. Now, right out of the north comes a wall of blue-black clouds. I'm driving south and the weather is behind me so I don't see it until the sun just goes *out*. Oh lord, it's a blue norther! Only in Texas! God, what terrifying weather! It gets so *cold* and dark within minutes. Rain comes down, hard. After twenty minutes of that, the dirt highway is just a sea of mud. I can't see. I pull over. I turn off the engine. No use wasting gas. I'm not going anywhere.

With the engine off, I hear a roaring sound up ahead. *What is that?* I think. Then I realize it's the Salt Fork of the Red

River, just north of Wellington. That peaceful, pretty river I've come to love is not peaceful today. Mabel and I have spent many summer afternoons here. The water's never higher than our ankles or knees. Now? With the rain, the river is flooded, but good.

I get out of the truck cab. I walk closer and the roar from the water gets louder. Another blast of wind and icy rain from the blue norther makes me shake. It's two in the afternoon, yet it is almost as dark as night, now. I get to the little bridge over the river and think *I'm not going to get home tonight.* The water from the river is already running *over* the bridge itself. It's not safe to cross. It's not the kind of bridge for a truck even on a sunny day. It's made for horses and wagons, not trucks. I drive over it oh-so-slow when I have to cross it. But today, only a crazy man would try to cross that bridge.

Unknown to me, Buddy Mills has been caught out in the same blue norther. He sees me pull over. He's driving his pa's older truck. He sees me, and wants to put the hurt on me. He kills his engine. He gets out of his pa's truck, takes off his belt with a heavy metal buckle on it. He pulls out a gun from under the truck seat. He sticks it into the back of his work pants. He walks up behind me. I'm not paying attention. I can only hear the roar of the river. All the while that blue norther puts its weird blue black darkness across the world.

Wham! Whap! Wham! I feel a terrible pain in the back of my head. I fall to the ground. I get up, all the while Buddy hitting me with his belt and that big, hard buckle. I see who it is. Without thinking I catch the belt before he can hit me again. I yank Buddy forward with the belt, then put my foot out so that he trips. Buddy's so surprised that he falls flat on his face. He's face down in mud and doesn't move for a minute. Then I see the gun stuck into the back of Buddy's pants. *My lord* I thought. *He means to kill me.* Buddy picks himself up, pulls out his gun. Now, I am running for my life.

CHAPTER 19

MY SECOND LIFE ENDS,
OCTOBER 31, 1926

I FIGHT FOR MY LIFE

I make for the river. I run along the raging water, as close as I can, without falling in. Falling into that…well, it would be death. No one can swim in water like that.

Soon, I think Buddy is a few minutes behind me. He's wearing big muddy farm boots on slow, heavy feet. He's angry. He's shouting. I can't hear what. I guess he can't run and shout at the same time. That's a good thing. It means I might stay ahead of him. I'm no great runner, but so far my legs are holding up. I run away from the highway where my truck is. I'm going over rough ground. I make my way ahead into brush, mud, rocks, the roar of the water always to my left. It's really dark now, but I know this area well. There are places to hide. I might get lucky.

Why? What is this big country boy so angry at? That a black man has a truck and he doesn't? Or is it just that I'm black? Does it matter now? He means to kill me, and it doesn't matter why. It's just like Tulsa! I am so afraid. There is no one to help me, now. There's no one out in a storm like this.

It's almost completely dark, but up ahead I see a band of five or six little trees. I get to them, and slip between them, into complete blackness. The branches of the trees overhead whip in the wind, just over my head. The roar of the river fills the air. Just let me rest. Just a few minutes. If I'm lucky, Buddy will give up. I can find a farmhouse nearby. Maybe get some help.

And just as I think that, here is Buddy. He's on me so fast I can hardly believe it! This time he doesn't use the belt. He has his gun. He points it at me, and shoots. BAM! My right shoulder is on fire! Oh god that hurts! Buddy drags me out of the trees, toward the wild river. I grab him with what little life I have left. We fight for the gun. We are right at the edge of that roaring water. He's strong, but he's surprised. He's a big heavy kid who is not used to someone fighting back. As we fight I hear his gun go off again. BLAM!

Buddy gets the strangest look of surprise on his face. Then Buddy falls backward. He screams as he goes. He's in the water. He's carried away in that fast, roaring water. I can see him trying to swim, but it's no good. He yells a few more times as he's swept away in the water. Then, all I can hear is the blue norther, the wind, and the river. I put my hand to my shoulder. It comes away red. My blood. Funny. I can't stand any more. I crawl back to the band of trees, away from the river, and into the darkness.

CHAPTER 20

IN BETWEEN

LUCKY JACK ENTRINGER

I seem to sleep for a while. Then I'm in a gray world. I feel no pain. I hear nothing. I'm lying on my back. Then I see trees above me. These aren't the little trees by the river. These trees are tall and reach out of sight into the darkness. It's not really dark up there, where surely the trees must reach the sky. No tree can go up forever. Instead I see thousands of little points of light, like stars. It's as though the tops of the trees, the dark sky, and heaven itself are one and the same.

I think, *I must be lying on my back if I'm looking up into the trees of heaven.* I laugh a little at that thought. I'm pretty sure I'm dead. Here I am, laying on my back and naming a new kind of tree. Pretty good for a dead guy.

I turn my head to the right and I see I am not alone. It's dark under these trees where I am. Yet the even darker shapes of four men are very clear. They seem to be sitting in chairs around a table. I can't see their faces, but I know they are looking at me. I'm not afraid. I just wonder why they are there, and why I am here.

Each man has a cup on the table. One man lifts his cup and

drinks from it. Then he does a strange thing. He stands up, and goes to each man. He picks up each man's cup and lifts it up so each one can drink. One of the men, after taking a drink, lifts his arm in thanks. The man who is helping him nods, *You're welcome.* Only then do I understand that the three men still sitting at the table have no hands. Their coat sleeves just end in darkness.

The man who is helping them comes over to me. I hear his shoes move through the soft sand. When he gets close enough he kneels down and looks into my face. He smiles and says, "Hey Maul, you've grown up." It's Lucky Jack Entringer.

CHAPTER 21

IN BETWEEN

UNCLE JACK TALKS

"Uncle Jack?" I say. I try to get up.

He pushes me back down very gently. He says, "Stay right where you are." He looks around, shakes his head. He says, "In this place, it's best you don't move around. I don't want you getting used to being here."

I have no idea what he's talking about. I lay back down. It's comfortable here on the soft sand, under those splendid tall trees that surely reach all the way to heaven.

I can't get over it. Here's my Uncle Jack. I've missed him so much! I have so much to tell him. He looks just as I'd seen him my last night in Tulsa. White shirt with dirt from the fire on it, dark slacks, good shoes…do I see blood on his shirt? He sees me looking and touches it. "Don't worry. Doesn't hurt. I got that my last night in Tulsa." He looks at me for a few minutes. He reaches down and touches my neck. He says, "I see you still have those ghost beads I gave you."

It's true. I can feel the little brown seed necklace against my skin.

"Ghost beads?" I ask.

"Yeah," Uncle Jack says. "I got them when I went west. Before you were born. They always brought me patience, and luck. They're from the cedar trees that grow out there. That's why they smell so good."

I ask, "Who are those men?" I nod toward the three men sitting at the table. They're just dark shapes in the gray. They sit still, the cups they can't pick up in front of them.

"I don't know," Uncle Jack says. "One speaks French. The other two speak Spanish. I can't speak either so I can't catch what they're telling me. I get the feeling they were traveling together out here. Oh, many years ago! They've been sitting there a long, long time. With those cups of wine in front of them and not able to drink."

"What happened to their hands?" I ask.

"Well," Uncle Jack says, "As near as I can make out, they got attacked and robbed one night. Whoever it was, killed them, then took their hands *and* their feet. I have no idea why someone would do that. Those poor guys, they can't walk anywhere and they can't drink anything."

CHAPTER 22

IN BETWEEN

UNCLE JACK TELLS ME WHAT TO DO

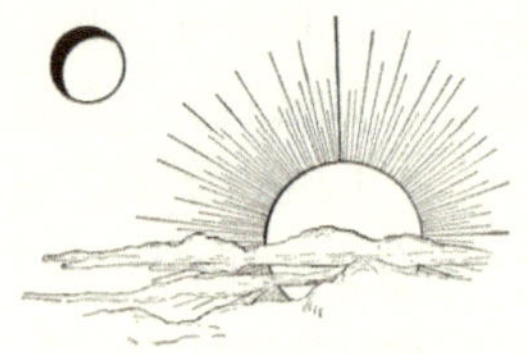

I try to sit up again. This time Uncle Jack lets me. He hugs me. He's warm. He feels real.

Uncle Jack says, "We need to get you out of here pretty soon. Get you back to where you need to go. You've got a third life coming. You need to get to where it begins."

I say, "What do I do? What do I do with a third life? I liked my *second* life! I want it back!"

Uncle Jack says, "Yeah, yeah, I get that. I'm not the one calling the shots here. On to a third life you must go."

I feel so sad. I cry silently. My Mabel. My dreams.

"You didn't get another life," I say.

"True enough," he says. A minute goes by. Then he says, "Now hold on. This is not the end. You need to change your plans a little, is all. Now listen. That man who shot you. I don't know where he's ended up."

"Is Buddy dead?" I ask.

"Was that his name?" Uncle Jack says. "That was one ugly white man. Oh yeah, he's dead. He's miles from where he fell in to the river. The flood waters have carried him far off. Before long, someone's going to find him. Word is going to get around that you were gone at the same time he went missing. If you go back home now with everyone knowing you two had hard feelings between you, the good white people in town will put you in jail. You'll never get out. It won't matter what you tell them, that he attacked you first. The fact is, some of them will even *believe* Buddy attacked you first. But you'll go to jail just the same."

"Why? Why? Why is this happening to me? All these mistakes! I didn't even know I was making them!" I cry. I pull sand and mud into my fists and hold it, so tight.

Uncle Jack lets me cry some more. Then he leans over to my ear and tells me what I need to do. He tells me I need to leave for a while. My truck is waiting for me by the road. I need to turn it around. I should drive west. I should plan to be gone for a few years. I can get my Mabel back, if I can wait.

He says, "You can write to your wife, tell her what happened. *In no way can she tell anyone she has heard from you!* She needs to tell people she's worried that your truck's been stolen, that you've been hurt. She needs to make a report to the sheriff."

Uncle Jack pats me on the shoulder. He eases me back down. When I'm laying down again, he says, "When you get out west, go to a town called Shiprock. You need to get you some new ghost beads. Some of the Indians out there will let you have some." He sighs. Then he says, "You need to find out how to live, get past all these terrible things that have happened to you. Mistakes, you say? Hear me then: THEY ARE NOT YOUR MISTAKES!"

His voice is so loud. I clap my hands over my ears and

close my eyes. I feel I am falling from a terrible height. Uncle Jack is gone; the handless, feetless, nameless men at the table are gone; the splendid tall trees with lights in the branches are gone.

CHAPTER 23

MY THIRD LIFE, NOVEMBER? 1926?

FIRST MORNING

I opened my eyes. It was bright. Everything was cold and clear to the eye. Each thing, a tree, a rock, a bird just above my face on a tree branch, was clear with deep color. Sometimes after it rains, you see these colors, this *realness*, the sharp shapes. That's the only way I can think to tell you about it.

Where was I? *When* was I? How long was I in between? *Who* was I? A new person, all over again? I sat up. Half a dozen little birds that had been sharing my resting place flew straight out into the cold morning air. I stood up on shaky legs. I stepped out from under a little band of short trees. I knew this place. I had run into the trees to hide from Buddy Mills.

I looked down at myself. I was covered in sand and mud. My feet were bare. Where were my shoes? My clothes were wrong. They were too loose. My pants hung down over my bare feet.

It was so cold! The eastern sky was getting light. It was about sunrise, I thought. I could see the black clouds of the blue norther moving away, to the south. Well, that answered one question—I had spent the night under the trees. The blue norther raged all night, then passed on its way, as such storms do. The river was down a little. It was still flooded, it was still talking, but it didn't have last night's *roar*.

My thoughts came in little bits and pieces. What…what? I had been *shot*. I quickly opened my too-long shirt to check my shoulder. There was no blood on my skin. I put my hand on my shoulder, expecting sharp pain. There was nothing. I pulled my shirt away and saw—nothing. My skin was smooth. How could that be? I had been shot. There had to be a wound, but there wasn't any sign of one.

The brown seed necklace was gone, too. I looked under the trees in the growing light, but there was no sign of the seeds, or the string that had held them together.

Suddenly I felt something like little stones in my mouth. I spat them out. The things flew out of my mouth and onto the wet ground. I picked up one. It was a *tooth*. I dropped it quickly. I had spat out three *teeth*. Were they mine? I felt inside my mouth with a finger. Three teeth on the right side were missing! But my mouth didn't hurt. I was as though I had lost those teeth months ago. Everything was healed. I couldn't understand any of it.

I felt my face and my head. I had a beard! It was long and thick. I had been clean shaven the day before, just how Mabel liked it. My hair was a mess, wet and sandy. It covered the back of my neck. I had had short hair just yesterday.

I suddenly had to sit down again. This was all too much. It had happened again! I died, and in coming back to life, I was changed. Shorter, thinner, missing three teeth, hair and beard so long. Was I older? Younger?

I needed to get to my truck. I needed to get warm. I needed

to see Mabel. I needed help. I was going to do exactly what Uncle Jack told me not to do. I was going home to my wife.

I made my way back to the highway. The river had gone down, for sure. The flood left behind fallen trees and oceans of mud. It took forever to get to the highway through all of that. Finally, I reached the truck. It was still there! It seemed fine. Even the cotton was still loaded in the back. I didn't see Buddy Mills' truck anywhere. I felt a little cold at that. Someone had already been by here, and seen my truck. Was it Mr. Mills, looking for his son?

I couldn't think about that right now. I got into the cab of my truck, and looked out the windshield ahead of me. Something was wrong. Something looked horribly different. I couldn't put it together. What was it? Then I saw what it was. Ahead, the bridge to Wellington was gone. The flood had taken it out.

CHAPTER 24

MY THIRD LIFE, NOVEMBER 1, 1926

A BROKEN BRIDGE

I cried out, "No! No no no!" I sat in my truck and put my face in my hands. I wasn't getting to Wellington any time soon. There was nowhere to cross the river. If this bridge was out, they would all be out, for miles on each side. It might take me days to find a way to cross.

My breathing slowed down. I had to think. I had to do something. I got out of my truck and walked up to what was left of the bridge. On the far side of the bridge I saw what had taken it out. Part of a house lay against the river bank. Someone had built their house too close to the river. The flood came, took the house, and then slammed it against the bridge. The bridge came down, and that was that. I was not going to get through. The river was still very high.

An idea came to me. I would turn around and drive north to Shamrock. I would drop off my load of cotton at the train station. One of the ranchers I knew, Mr. Wright, lived not too far away. It was on my way to Shamrock! He might help me, if I didn't look *too* different. If I looked even a little like the Maul Entringer he knew, it might be enough.

I got back into my truck. I saw something on the floor of the cab on the passenger side. Odd. I hadn't put anything there the day before. With all I had been through, being attacked, getting shot, dying, seeing my years-dead Uncle Jack, and coming back to a third life...*nothing* would surprise me now. I looked close. It was a pair of men's shoes, a very good pair. They were brown, and looked almost new. I picked the shoes up. Size 8 1/2. Under them on the cab floor were footprints made of water, in the shape of the shoes. I put the shoes back down, gently, hardly breathing. The shoes were not mine. I was a size 10. Something told me they would fit if I tried them on. I turned my truck around and headed north.

I found Mr. Wright up and beginning his ranch work. It took him a minute to recognize me. "Is it....Maul?" he asked, after a minute.

"Yes sir, Mr. Wright," I said. "Got caught in the flood."

Looking at my long beard and hair, Mr. Wright said, "I see. The Salt Fork flooded, did it?" He looked at my wet, muddy clothes.

"Yes sir," I said. "The bridge is out."

"Oh?" he said.

"Hit by a house that washed away, looks like," I said.

"Well," Mr. Wright said after a minute, "You might not be getting home any time soon. Let me get you some clothes to change into. You know where the water pump is. You might wash up a bit." Then he left.

I went out to the pump next to the barn. I hated to do it, it was so cold, but I pumped water and did my best to wash away most of the mud. My feet were really bad.

Mr. Wright came out of the house and laid out some old, clean pants and socks. There was a shirt and a jacket on top, and, of all things, a pair of scissors. He said, "Thought you could use the scissors, too. There's a mirror just inside the barn." He went back into the house to let me dress.

CHAPTER 25

MY THIRD LIFE, NOVEMBER 1, 1926

MRS. WRIGHT MAKES BREAKFAST

It was heaven to put on warm, clean clothes. The air was still cold from the blue norther. It would stay cold for a few days, now, because of the storm. I went to the truck to put on the socks. I put on the brown shoes I had found, Size 8 1/2. Sure enough, they fit perfectly. Yesterday, they would have been too small. Today, they fit. So my feet were smaller, too. I would find more little changes as the days passed. I had a white scar on my right hand that I didn't have before. My right eye watered a lot at the end of a long day of driving. All of that was new.

I went to the mirror in the barn and used the scissors to cut away my long hair. I cut my beard as close as I could to my face. Until I could shave, it was the best I could do.

Mr. Wright called from outside the barn, "Got something for you to eat. Mrs. Wright wants you to eat before you go."

I went out to find a plate of biscuits and a cup of milk. I had the food and the delicious warm milk gone in about 30 seconds. The first meal in my third life was a wonder. It was simple and delicious as only country food can be. It was also the last breakfast I would have in Texas for eight years.

I didn't find Mr. Wright anywhere. He must have gone back into his house, and I felt shy about knocking on his door. With the way I looked, he must have been pretty shocked. I checked in my truck cab for my money box. It was still there, under the seat! I took out a dollar and left it under a rock at the water pump. I drove away, back out to the highway. I got to the train station at Shamrock and unloaded the cotton.

The freight worker at the station said, "Must have rained where you were."

"Yes, sir, it did," I answered.

In Shamrock I found a general store. I parked in back by the "colored entrance" and went in. I bought new pants, a new shirt, a cap, and a thick jacket. I also bought a razor, soap, and towels so I could shave. The store had a few customers, and I had to wait to pay. Two sheriff's deputies from Shamrock jail came in to talk to the store owner.

One of them said, "Yeah, we're on our way to help out the sheriff in Wellington. They've had a flood and there's been dead bodies found. They think one's the son of a farmer down there."

The other deputy pushed his hat back on his head. He looked at me. I kept my eyes down and pretended to look at the things I'd bought. I turned to look at some soap, acting as if I'd forgotten to buy any. I got back in line. By the time I'd done that, the sheriff's deputies had gone.

I paid for my things and left the store. I got in my truck. My hands were shaking. My inside was as cold as ice. Tears streamed down my face. I remembered what Uncle Jack told me. I couldn't go back to Wellington. No matter what I said, I would go to jail. A new thought came to me *You won't just go to jail. You might be killed.* Mabel *might be killed. Look what happened in Tulsa.* I needed to get out of here. I needed to run.

I turned my truck to the west and I drove all day and into the next night.

That was the first day of my third life.

CHAPTER 26

MY THIRD LIFE, 1926-1934
THE SHERIFF OF TUCUMCARI

I crossed into New Mexico, west of Texas. In Tucumcari, just over the state line, I lived in my truck for a while. I stayed near Tucumcari's brand-new train station and took whatever trucking jobs I could find. No one really grew anything out there. It wasn't like Oklahoma or Texas. New Mexico was dry, and mostly mountains. There weren't as many people. It got very, very cold at night.

Mostly I took tourists around the area. They came in a train from Chicago or Kansas City or New York and they wanted to look around. Once I took a pair of photographers around. I had a few bales of hay I was trucking from one farmer to another, and the photographers enjoyed sitting on the hay bales in the back of the truck. They said it gave them a better view of the "big landscape," as they called it. After that I always kept a few hay bales in back. I could always sell them, if I needed to. Ranchers' horses, cattle, or sheep needed to eat.

I hardly noticed the big landscape, the mountains, the desert, the amazing colors. I stayed locked into the idea that I had to run. That I would go to jail. That everyone I cared about would disappear or die. I slept and ate poorly. Nothing tasted good.

I was sleeping out in my truck one early December night in a small park near the train station when the sheriff of Tucumcari woke me up. I sat up, my heart pounding, my hands up like someone was pointing a gun at me. Was he going to take me off to jail? Had he heard about a murdered farmer's son far off in West Texas? Instead, he was kind.

He said, "You're all right. Calm down." He looked at me a minute, then said, "You know, it's going to get a lot colder than it is now. You're going to need to find a place to stay. I don't want to come by here and find you frozen to death."

I had been cold and sleeping badly, and I had been wondering what to do. I couldn't think of where to live. There really weren't many black people here. I didn't know where I *could* live. What if Tucumcari was like Garnet, where blacks could only live in The Flats?

I took a deep breath to calm myself. Then I said, "Thank you for your concern, sir. Can you suggest a place?"

He liked my polite tone, I guess. He said, "Just down that road is a house." He pointed. "A family has it. The family's called Hernandez. I know they've got an empty room in back. The guy who was there left town on the morning train without paying rent. Have you got money to show them?"

I nodded my head. He nodded back and said, "All right. Just give them two weeks' rent in cash and they'll be happy to have you. You might be able to park your truck behind their place. What's your name, anyway?"

Without thinking too hard about it, I said, "Jack Johnson." Jack for my Uncle Jack, and Johnson for my Mabel. Before marrying me, she was Mabel Johnson.

"All right, Jack. Take care then, and don't let me find you

sleeping out here again," the sheriff said. We looked at each other in the darkness. Then he asked, "Were you in the Great War?" He thought I had been in the 1917 war against Germany. Did I look that old?

"No sir, I was not," I said.

"Huh," he said. "The way you woke up reminds me of a couple of guys I know who were in the war. They came back changed men. Well…take care of yourself. Get you to the Hernandez's place and see if they can't rent you a room. If Maria Hernandez asks if you want meals as well as the room, say 'yes.' She's a good cook." Then he walked away into the night.

CHAPTER 27
MY THIRD LIFE, 1926-1934
MABEL

As soon as I could I wrote a letter to Mabel in Wellington, telling her what happened. I asked her to tell no one about Buddy Mills. I told her I would write her again soon. I gave my address as "Jack Johnson, General Delivery, Tucumcari, New Mexico." Two weeks later, the letter was returned with "Return to Sender, Address not Known" stamped on it. We hadn't lived in Wellington long. We hadn't made any friends yet so there was no one I could send the letter to, instead. I then had the idea to send the letter to the hospital where she worked. Two more weeks went by, then three weeks, and then a month went by. A second month went by. No letter from Mabel.

Before long, I drove south. I spent the rest of the winter in Santa Rosa, where it was warmer. I wrote Mabel again, and waited for an answer. None came.

When I think about my third life, I can think only of confusion, sadness, and fear. My memories were of a man who had lost his chance in life. I moved from town to town, from Santa Rosa to Albuquerque to Santa Fe and back to Albuquerque.

Albuquerque is where I stayed the longest. I made money trucking, picking up what work I could. They had a big train yard there and lots of freight moved through it.

It was in Albuquerque that I finally heard from Mabel. I sat in my little rented room, and read her letter. She said she had done as I asked. She had reported me missing to the sheriff in Wellington. Yes, Buddy Mills' body had been found. He had been caught in the flood and drowned, everyone said. No one said anything about him being shot.

Then Mabel wrote something I never thought would come from her. She wrote, "No one has said anything about you and Buddy Mills. I don't think anyone here thinks you hurt him. I want you back here with me. We'll make up some story about why you've been gone. If you really are the man I married, if you really love me, you'll come back now." She had signed the letter "Mabel Entringer." Not "Love, Mabel" or "Your wife, Mabel" or even just "Mabel."

She had just asked me to do the one thing I could not do. I could not go back to Wellington. She had no idea how bad things could get.

CHAPTER 28

MY THIRD LIFE, 1926-1934
THE GREAT DEPRESSION

Life got a lot harder once the Great Depression came in '29. I lived in rented rooms, and when I was short of money, I slept in my truck. Whatever money I had, I put back into my truck. I learned to repair it myself. It was a good truck to begin with, and I took care of it. My hair and beard still grew crazy fast. I had to cut my hair once every two weeks, and shave twice a day. Sometimes, I'd scatter my long black hair outdoors into the wind. I don't know why.

I sent letters to Mabel, lots of them. I told her about Tulsa and the burning of Greenwood. I told her how my Uncle Jack had died, and how I had lost Ma, Pa, Teeny, and Ulysses. I tried to explain how bad things could get if I returned to Wellington. In my last letter to her I asked if she would leave Wellington. Could she meet me in another city? We could start a new life together.

Mabel never answered. Something inside me got smaller, and became hard. The years crept forward. I just breathed and lived and ate and slept, and not much more. I didn't plan anything, and I didn't look forward to anything much.

In December, 1933, I was in Farmington, in the northwest corner of the state. There wasn't enough work for me there. I was planning to drive back to Albuquerque, where there might be more work. I wanted to get there before it started to snow hard in the mountains. I wouldn't be able to drive through after that happened.

The night before I was to leave, I went to the town square to walk. It was dark and cold, but the townspeople had put up lights and candles in the downtown. Everyone was out walking, and dressed up in their warm winter coats. A small Mexican band played. Their singer, a young boy, sang a pretty tune in Spanish.

Some of the shops were open and their bright lights shone out on the square. You could smell the smoke from dozens of wood fires. The smell was deep and sweet, like pine trees or cedars. The smell started me thinking. For the first time in months, I thought of the ghost beads Lucky Jack Entringer had given me the last night of his life. I'd worn them my entire second life. By the first morning of my third life, they were gone. Without knowing it, I had missed having the warm-feeling little brown seeds against my skin. They had that same deep pine smell I was smelling now on Farmington's town square. What had my Uncle Jack said as I lay by the side of the Salt Fork of the Red River? What? What had he said? It seemed important. It was a town's name. A strange little name. He said I should go there.

CHAPTER 29
MY THIRD LIFE, 1926-1934
GHOST BEADS

I stopped walking as memories and thoughts overcame me. I found myself in a quiet corner of the town square. Hardly anyone was there. In front of me, an old Indian man had spread a blanket on the ground. He was selling some beautiful silver pieces, bracelets and rings, that I would never have money for. He was sitting very still in the cold in the center of the blanket. I walked over and said hello. Without looking up, he nodded a greeting. To be polite, I looked at the things he was selling.

I felt a strange movement in the air, as though a bird had flown right by my head. I looked around in surprise. The old man had moved to a wooden chair at the back of the blanket. How had he done that? He had moved fast, and silently. I looked closer at him. He wasn't as old as I had first thought. His hair was black now, and tied back. His hands, now resting on his knees, looked like those of a younger man, no more than 40. Something else was different. He was looking straight at me. I looked straight back.

After a long moment I asked him where he was from. In a

pleasant voice, he said, "Shiprock." And then I remembered what Uncle Jack had said. He told me I should go to Shiprock and get some ghost beads. He had said: *I got them when I went west. Before you were born. They always brought me patience, and luck.*

I felt excited. I don't know why. It was like finding out the end of story you wanted to know about, or learning a reason for something that happened that you had never understood.

Hardly able to speak, I asked the man, "Do you have any ghost beads?" Now it was his turn to look surprised.

He answered, "That's not what most people ask for. Maybe I have some. My aunt makes them. Hold on."

I looked around the town square while he felt around in his sacks and boxes for the ghost beads. He made a sound like *Ah!* and I looked back at him. Once again he had changed places without my hearing or seeing him make the change. He was sitting once again in the center of his blanket. The chair was gone. *Now*, he was no more than 18 years old! I stepped back. "What?" I said, after a minute.

He said, in a young man's voice, "I'm not the only one doing that, you know. Ever since you came on the town square, I've been watching you change. You started out at about 17, maybe? Then you looked 30, and big. And now...," he stopped talking. He handed me a string of dark brown seeds. He said, "Are these what you're looking for mister?"

They were ghost beads. I rubbed them between my fingers. They gave off that beautiful cedar smell. I can't remember how much he asked for them. I just handed over the money. Then I slipped them over my head and gently pushed them inside my shirt, against my skin. I told the young man good-bye.

That night, for the first time since I'd come to Farmington, it rained. I heard it on the roof of the little room I had rented. The next morning I got up to leave. Outside my door was a tiny gray kitten, completely wet and shivering. Without much thought I picked her up, dried her off, and put her inside my coat to warm up. I drove away, out of Farmington. On my first night out I found a farmer who had some warm milk to sell. I drank some, and gave the rest to the kitten, who drank a dish of it in minutes. That was Mew.

CHAPTER 30

MY THIRD LIFE, 1926-1934
DARK NIGHT

It took me from December, 1933 to June, 1934 to get back to the river bank where my second life ended and my third life began. It was hard to find work. I could only go as far as I could and still make money for gas, and food. I moved from town to town, looking for trucking work. There were terrible dust storms the closer to Texas I got. Twice I had to stop for a week or more and get inside somewhere until the storm was over.

During the second big dust storm, I had to stay in a farmer's barn. By then, Mew was learning to hunt. She would disappear at night. Every morning, though, she would be curled up on the blanket near me. Sometimes she would bring me the present of a mouse.

During one very bad night when the dust was black and everywhere, and you could not see outside at all, Mew stayed close. I stayed awake all night. The wind was strong and sounded like voices. The smell of dust was strong. As I lay in the darkness, I came to understand that my whole life—all three of them—was not completely mine. Whatever good memories I had, playing as a child, eating Ma's good cooking, talking with my friend Chester Hollis, meeting Mabel and marrying her and laying with her under a tree by the river, had been covered, like black dust, with *bad memory*.

I don't mean "bad memories." I mean bad *memory*. There are memories, and there is *memory*. "What?" you ask. I'll tell you. You take your mother's lunch, which might be a nice juicy apple. You hurt her feelings and then feel sorry about it. That is one bad memory. You act up in school, and your teacher hits your hand hard and gives you a talking to. You might not be sorry, but that is another bad memory. Those then, are memories.

But when I talk about bad *memory*, I mean something different. You make a mistake. Maybe it seems small. Or not like a mistake at all. It's just a white girl in an elevator when you forget to get off. Then, what happens to you is so bad, you can't ever forget it. It makes a mark on you. It changes what you do for the rest of your life. That is bad memory.

Then maybe a second mistake is waiting for you. That one, too, might seem small. It's ignoring a white man who is angry at his pa. You are just standing there like a target for someone to hit, attack, or shoot. Maybe at the time you *do* know it's a mistake, but you can't change anything, because of bad memory. Because of that first mistake. It's like you are frozen. You are filled with bad memory and the new mistake rolls right past you like a train, and takes everything away. That is what I'm saying now.

I can't change the first mistake. I ran, after that one. Sure, Mr. Greene and Uncle Jack helped me run. They knew I couldn't stay. I was young, just 17. If the wrong men had found me, they would have killed me no matter what my age.

But now I think the second mistake, in 1926, I didn't have

to make. Oh, I had to disappear. I needed to go. That is clear. You don't kill a white man and stay around. Not if you're black. No, the mistake was staying gone for seven years. I left my wife Mabel. I let her leave *me*. I let her go. I wandered around feeling nothing, enjoying nothing, and letting my frozen life, and my love for my wife, slip right through my fingers. These were my thoughts as I lay in a barn in Clovis, New Mexico, the night outside black with dust and the endless wind.

What I came to understand that dark and endless night in Clovis was enough to help me pass the New Mexico/Texas state line. I drove through Texas, ready to run at the first sign of a sheriff. My hands hurt from holding the steering wheel of my truck so hard. Mew slept peacefully on her blanket in the cab next to me.

CHAPTER 31

MY THIRD LIFE, JUNE 20, 1934
I GET IN MY TRUCK AND GO

I stand here now on a cool summer morning in West Texas. I've spent the night at the same spot where my second life ended and my third life began. I slept well. There were no dreams, and no ghosts. Wherever Buddy Mills ended up, it is far from here.

I'm on the highway to Wellington. I've crossed the new bridge on the Salt Fork of the Red River. It's big and well made. No flood will take that bridge out. I've stopped my old truck and gotten out. I look out into new sunshine. My heart is beating so hard I can hardly breathe. I have just a few more miles to go to town. Will someone recognize me? Call the sheriff? Will I find Mabel before that happens? I'm so afraid. I hope Mabel is there. Will she know who I am? Have I changed that much? Can I make her fall in love with me again even if I'm not the man she thought she had married? If I can have just that, that one important thing, then I will go look for my ma and pa. I'll find them, no matter where they are.

Mew sits on her blanket and looks at the road ahead. I have to go now. I get in my truck, and I go.

EPILOGUE

After many more miles in his Model-T truck, Maul found Mabel in Excelsior Springs, Missouri. Mabel had left Wellington. She had moved back to Missouri in the winter of 1934. She knew Maul right away. Winning over Mabel's father, Dr. Johnson, was another matter. Knowing what you know about Maul Entringer, do you think he gave up?

The Three Lives of Maul Entringer picks up the story of the husband of Mabel Entringer, a character in *The Visitors*, a story set in a Depression-era town in the Texas Panhandle. In *The Visitors*, we learned that Mabel's husband, a truck driver who owned his own truck, had disappeared in 1926, and was never heard from again. One reader of *The Visitors* told me she feared something terrible had happened to Maul Entringer, and that perhaps he had been killed and his truck stolen. Given the time (the 1920s) and the place (the American South) this was a reasonable fear. Maul Entringer was African American and was living in a dangerous and difficult time for African Americans and, really, anyone who was not white. I agreed with my reader that something seriously bad had happened to Maul in 1926 to make him disappear, but I wanted to examine all the possibilities. What emerged in my fictional world was that Maul Entringer was alive, but that tragic events in his youth had made him run after his disappearance in 1926. In other words, Maul had been traumatized by his past and could not deal with yet another threat to his life. His life was pushed completely off-course as a result.

What might have traumatized a young Maul Entringer so badly? I felt the Tulsa Race Riots of 1921 would qualify. Over the course of a few days beginning May 30, 1921, white mobs terrorized, beat, and shot African Americans after a young white woman accused a young black man of attacking her in an elevator. Even though the police stated no attack had taken place, mobs of white men acted out on their negative assumptions about young black men. The district where African Americans lived in Tulsa, called Greenwood, was completely burned including homes, schools, churches, and businesses. It is estimated that as many as 200 African Americans were killed, although the official count is much lower. African Americans and also whites lost up to $1.5 million dollars in destroyed property. That would be $22.8 million dollars today. Tulsa, Oklahoma, was already a dangerous "oil boom" town, but the race riots were truly violent, and a black spot on the history of the region. In today's terms the events in Tulsa were hate crimes committed on a large scale. By putting a 17-year-old Maul Entringer in the elevator with the young white woman, I created the basis for Maul's traumatic past.

The towns in Oklahoma, Texas, and New Mexico where Maul Entringer lives out three lives are all real, although one of them has been given a fictional name. Wherever possible I drew on authentic sources and created settings for Maul's lives that are as rooted in fact and local histories as I could make them. Everything else, other than the basic factual events of Tulsa, is fiction.

"Ghost Beads" are berries from the juniper tree strung together as protection against evil. As Navajo (Dine') historian Wally Brown says, juniper berries are used in the traditional

"Enemy Way" ceremony to help those who suffer from bad memory, in other words, those who have been in war or have experienced trauma. As Mr. Brown notes, we call this PTSD today, or Post Traumatic Stress Disorder. Mr. Brown is specific in his use of the term *bad memory* with *memory* in the singular form. See his video at: https://www.youtube.com/watch?v=F7XkcUBUs3w

For information and help for PTSD, see the National Alliance for Mental Health website at:

https://www.nami.org/About-Mental-Illness/Mental-Health-Conditions/Posttraumatic-Stress-Disorder/Support

I consulted many sources for this story, including:

- Alexander, C. (1995). *The Ku Klux Klan in the southwest.* Norman, OK: University of Oklahoma Press.
- Craven, J. (1969, March 27). Interview by Robert L. Foster [Tape recording]. Southwest Collection/Special Collections Library. Texas Tech University. Lubbock, Texas.
- Eubank, G. (1969, April 16). Interview by Robert L. Foster [Tape recording]. Southwest Collection/Special Collections Library. Texas Tech University. Lubbock, Texas.
- Ford, V. (1969, April 15). Interview by Robert L. Foster [Tape recording]. Southwest Collection/Special Collections Library. Texas Tech University. Lubbock, Texas.
- Foster, R.L. (1974). *Black Lubbock: A history of negroes in Lubbock, Texas, to 1940.* M.A. Thesis, Texas Tech University, Lubbock, Texas.

- Gorsuch, J.W. (Personal communication, November 11, 2020)
- Graves, A. (1969, April 8). Interview by Robert L. Foster [Tape recording]. Southwest Collection/Special Collections Library. Texas Tech University. Lubbock, Texas.
- Iles, O. (1969, March 24). Interview by Robert L. Foster [Tape recording]. Southwest Collection/Special Collections Library. Texas Tech University. Lubbock, Texas.
- Pioneer Business Development LLC (2018). *The bridge: A piece of Collingsworth County history* [DVD]. Wellington, TX.
- Tatum, M. (1969, April 24). Interview by Robert L. Foster [Tape recording]. Southwest Collection/Special Collections Library. Texas Tech University. Lubbock, Texas.
- Williams, L &. Williams, E. (1972). *Anatomy of four race riots*. Jackson, MS: University and College Press of Mississippi.

I wish to thank Mr. Randy Vance and Mr. James Marshall of the Southwest Collection/Special Collection Library for their patient help. Thanks always to my father, Mr. John Gorsuch, for his answers to my endless questions about trucks of the 1920s and 1930s, and his perspectives on life in the 1930s.

BOOKS IN THIS SERIES

American Chapters books by Greta Gorsuch

- *The Bee Creek Blues & Meridian*
- *Lights at Chickasaw Point & The Two Garcons*
- *Living at Trace*
- *Summer in Cimarron & Lunch at the Dixie Diner*
- *The Storm*
- *Cecilia's House & The Foraging Class*
- *The Visitors*

Ebooks and paperbacks are available from your favorite online retailer. Paperbacks may also be ordered by any bookstore, using the ISBN 978-1938757785. For more information, including store links, please see our website at

http://wayzgoosepress.com/greta-gorsuch